THE LION AND THE GYPSY

GEOFFREY PATTERSON

DOUBLEDAY
NEW YORK   LONDON   TORONTO
SYDNEY   AUCKLAND

Once there was a gypsy who lived in a land where the sun always shone. He traveled far and wide, but he never left the sound of the sea that he loved. Most of all he liked to sit and watch the waves as they rose and fell.

One day he said to himself, "It's been years and years since I saw my mother and father." And he felt a great longing to be with them again.

His old parents lived far away in a little village by the sea. The gypsy knew that if he walked far enough, with the sea at his right hand and the mountains at his left hand, he would come to them.

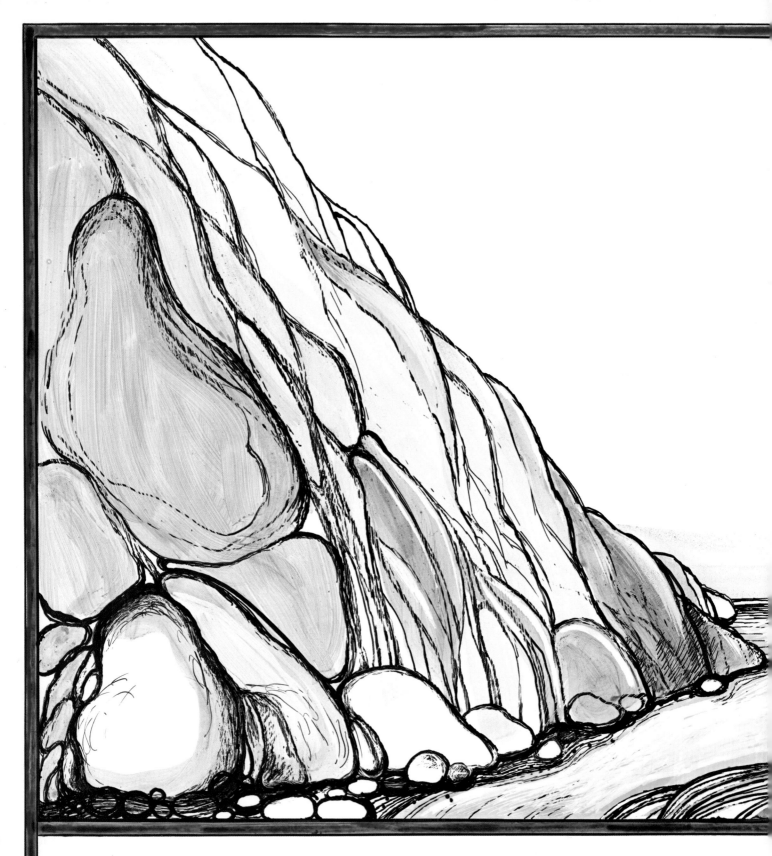

The very next day the gypsy set off. He wore his long robe of many colors that his mother had made for him, and over his head he wore a scarf the color of lemons, woven in silk, to shield him from the scorching sun. He took little else except the lute his father had given him when he was a boy.

Day after day he walked.
The white sand stretched out before him mile after mile. The mountains, the color of lavender and faded cornflowers, shimmered in the haze.
The sea sparkled like sapphires and diamonds under the cloudless sky.

Each day the gypsy walked until the sun set and the moon rose up into the night sky like a huge plate. Then he wrapped his robe around him to keep warm, and played his lute. This music reminded him of his parents and of his happy times with them as a boy.

On the evening of the seventh day the gypsy sat down to play as usual, but this time he was not alone.

Behind him, in the shadow of the rocks, sat a huge lion with a flowing golden mane. The lion listened to the beautiful music late into the night, until the gypsy stopped playing and fell asleep.

Only then did the lion come out of his hiding place. He walked up to the sleeping gypsy and gazed at him, wondering who he was and where he was going.

Then the lion went away, swishing his long tail on the sand to wipe out his paw prints, so the gypsy never knew he had been there.

For three days and three nights the lion followed the gypsy. And each night a new friend joined him to listen to the beautiful music—first the gray ibis bird, then the black scorpion, and last the green snake. They all listened in the shadows and the gypsy never knew they were there.

When he fell asleep, they came down to the seashore to watch over him and make sure he was safe for the night. But he never knew they were there.

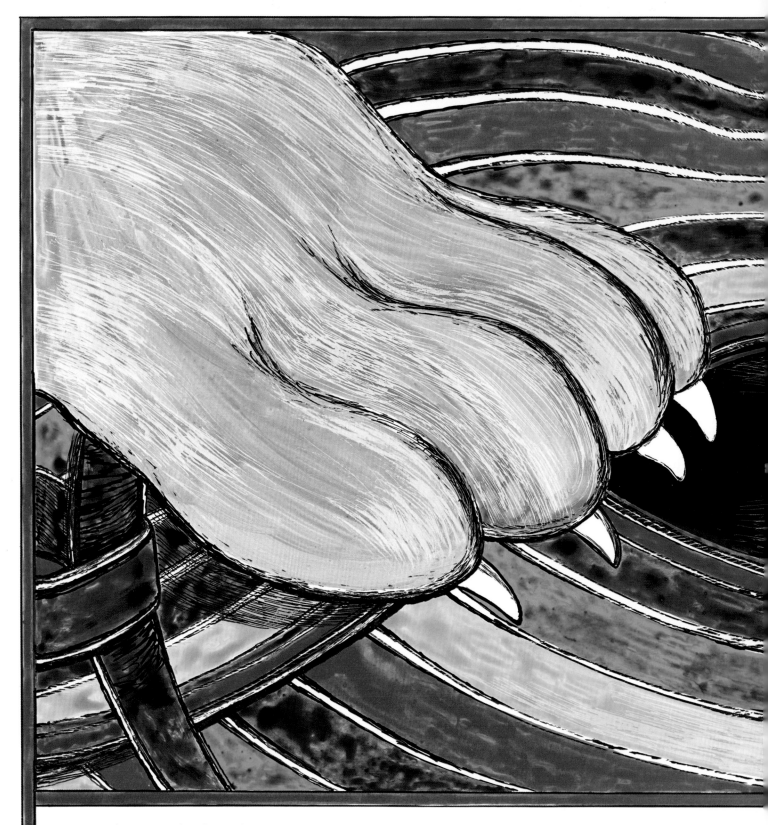

Then on the fourth morning something terrible happened. The gypsy did not wake up. The dawn came, the sun rose into the sky, but the gypsy lay by the sea with the sun beating down.

The lion and the other creatures crept up to him, but his eyes were closed, even when the lion gently touched him with his great paw.

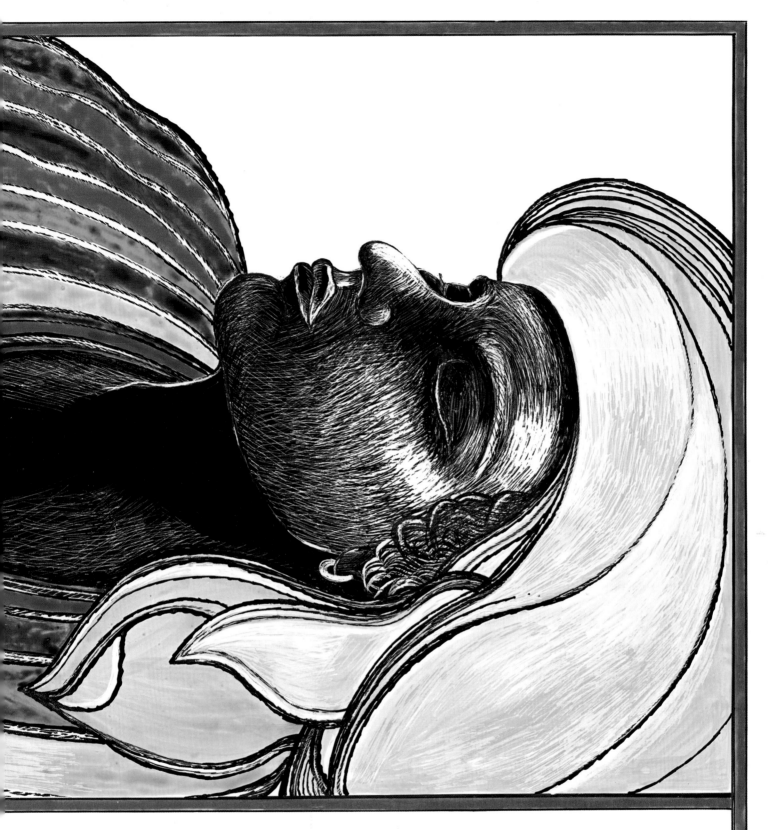

"What is wrong?" hissed the snake, slithering over the gypsy's feet.
"Why doesn't he wake up?" crackled the scorpion.
"Perhaps the heat is too much for him," said the ibis.

The lion drew close, and looked into the gypsy's still face for a long time.
"Something is wrong," he growled softly, "but I do not know what it is."
Then the ibis saw a fish lying by the gypsy's hand.
"I know that fish," he said. "It is the poisonous blowfish. The gypsy has
eaten it, and it has made him very ill."

They all looked at the ibis and then at the gypsy.
"If we leave him here he will die," said the ibis.
"Perhaps the lion could carry him," suggested the snake.
"No, no, he's too big," growled the lion.
"Well, why don't we take his lute instead?" said the little black
scorpion. "Someone is bound to recognize it."

But when the ibis tried to fly with the lute, it was too heavy. "You will have to carry it," said the ibis to the lion. "Only you are strong enough."

"I will try," said the lion, "but how will it stay on my back?"

"I will wrap myself round the lute and round you, and hold tight,"
said the snake.
"Very well," growled the lion. "But if you squeeze too hard, snake,
I'll bite your head off, so be careful."

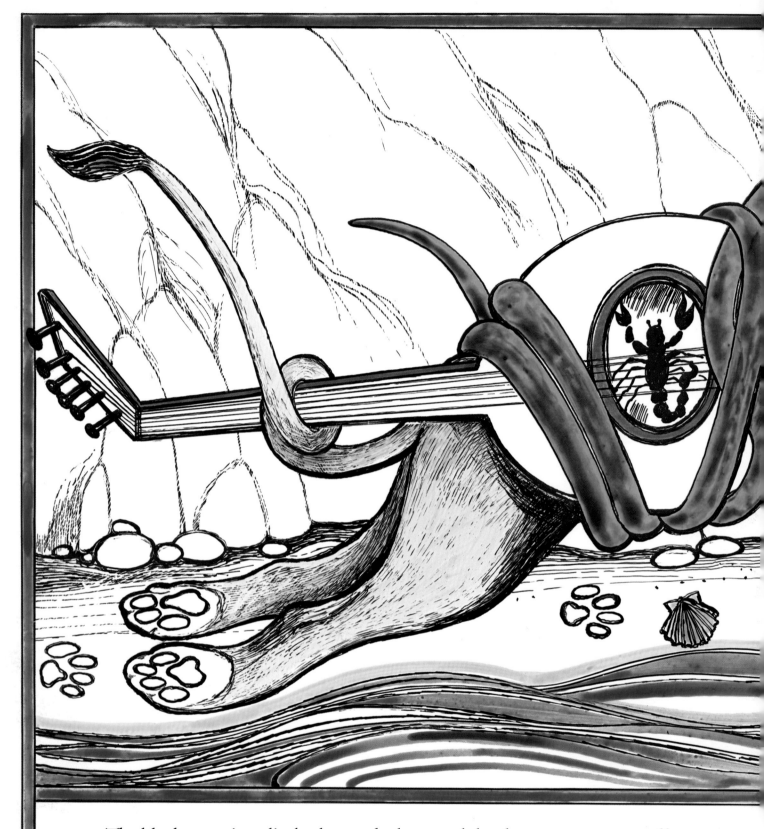

The black scorpion climbed onto the lute, and the three creatures set off
down the shore, leaving the gray ibis with his wings outstretched over
the gypsy.

The lion was indeed strong and very fast. His long flowing mane swept back
over his shoulders in the warm air as he raced along the sand.

The scorpion disappeared inside the lute to shelter from the sun, the snake held tight, but not too tight, and the lion ran faster and faster. Mile after mile of white sand passed under his huge paws as he ran, with the sea to his right and the mountains to his left.

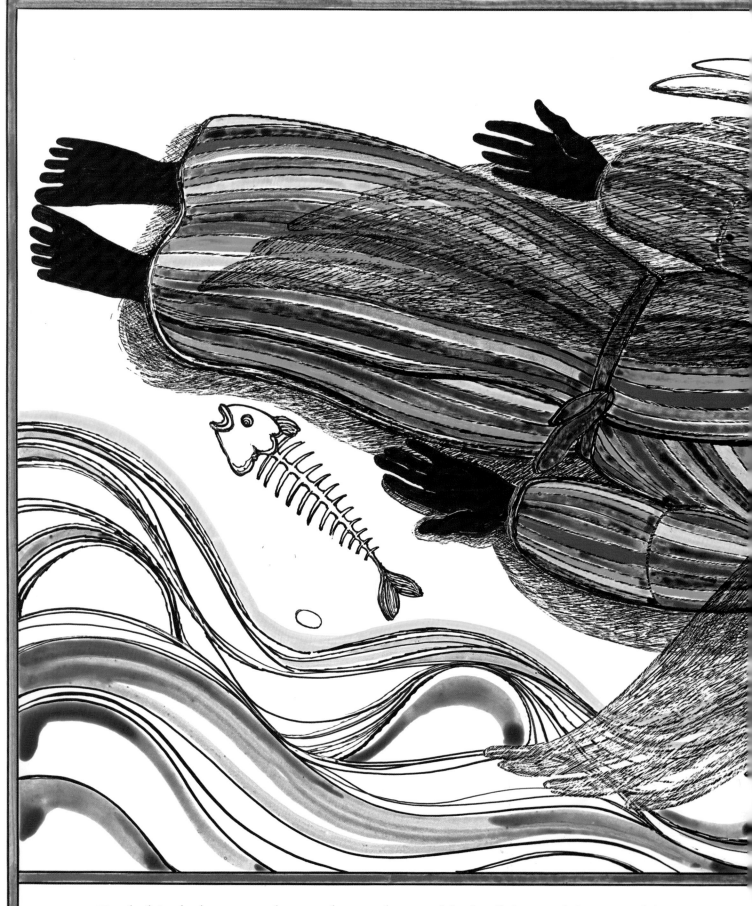

Far behind, the gypsy lay on the seashore with the ibis watching over him.

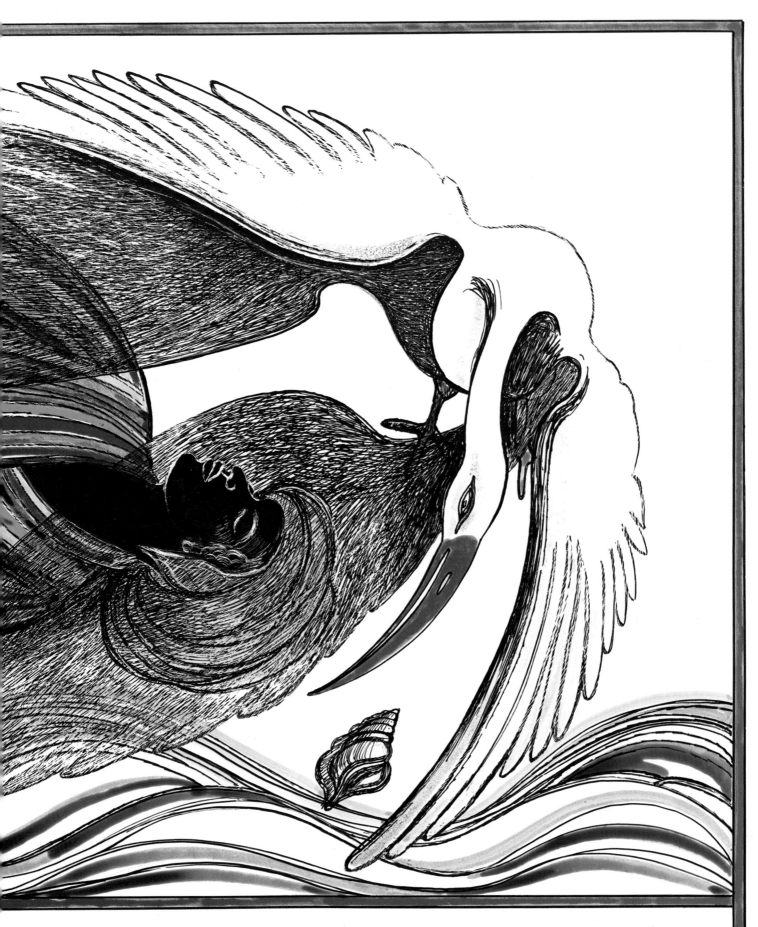

There was no sound, except for the crashing of the waves on the white sand.

As the sun began to sink in the sky, the lion grew tired and ran more slowly.
In the distance he could see a small village, and by the time he reached the edge
of the village he could go no farther.

The lion and the snake, both exhausted, fell asleep. But the little black scorpion crawled out of the lute and started to pluck the strings with his pincers.

The music drifted on the quiet evening air.
At the first house in the village, an old man and his wife heard it and
stopped to listen.
"That sounds like our son's lute," said the man in astonishment.

They followed the music, and soon found the sleeping lion and snake, and the little black scorpion playing the lute.

"What does this mean?" whispered the man.

"These beautiful animals have come to tell us our son is in trouble," said his wife.

And so they set out, following the lion's paw marks, with the sea on their left and the mountains on their right, until they found their son, with the ibis still watching over him.

They made a stretcher of driftwood from the sea, and with the lion's help they brought the gypsy back home to get well.

Each day the gypsy got better, and each day he would sit up in his bed under the palm tree beside the sea, and play his lute. The lion, the snake, and the ibis came to listen, and so did the little black scorpion.

Only this time the gypsy knew that they were there, and was glad to share his music and his happiness.

FOR HELEN NAPPER

PUBLISHED BY DOUBLEDAY
a division of Bantam Doubleday Dell Publishing Group, Inc.
666 Fifth Avenue, New York, New York 10103

DOUBLEDAY
and the portrayal of an anchor with a dolphin
are trademarks of Doubleday, a division of
Bantam Doubleday Dell Publishing Group, Inc.

Library of Congress Cataloging-in-Publication Data
Patterson, Geoffrey.
The lion and the gypsy / Geoffrey Patterson. — 1st ed. in the
U.S.A.
p.   cm.
Summary: Attracted by his beautiful lute playing, a group of
animals follows a traveling gypsy with great affection, even saving
his life at a critical time. The story was inspired by Rousseau's
painting "The Sleeping Gypsy."
[1. Gypsies—Fiction. 2. Animals—Fiction.] I. Title.
PZ7.P27647Li 1991
ISBN 0-385-41535-4
ISBN 0-385-41536-2 (lib. bdg.)
RL: 3.4